# DUCK'S KEY WHERE CAN IT BE?

Jez Alborough



Kane/Miller
BOOK PUBLISHERS

I've lost the key
to drive my truck.

Is it in the flowerpot?

Is it underneath the mat?

Is it in the mailbox then?

The back of the truck, it must be here...

Yoo-hoo Duck!

Did somebody whisper? Who could it be?

I think I'll look in here and see...